TABLE FOR TWO

* * * * * * * * * * *

At Least Got Us A Seat

Donna and Arnie Gilson

****

Julia Montgomery was pulling into the local shopping mall parking lot heading for her favorite restaurant. She parked at the nearest spot she could find, which was about five spaces away.

She switched off her ignition, put the book she had started reading into her purse and got out of her car. She was looking forward to a quiet meal and reading more into her book.

When she got out, she pushed the lock button on her remote and listened for the quick 'beep'. Her father always cautioned to do that. She smiled and headed for the restaurant.

Bob Warren was also pulling into the same parking lot. He was new in town and had spotted the same restaurant and decided he would try it.

He opened his car door stepped out and pushed the door lock button on the inside door panel. He had been told that if you used your remote; the signal could be read by someone watching with a special device and be able to unlock the doors.

As he backed away, he took a good look at his shiny new car. He had purchased it just before he left his last job. "Nice" he was thinking, then spotted a speck of dust.

"How dare that!" he actually said aloud then wiped it away. He then started for the restaurant.

As it turned out, both Julia and Bob met at the door the same time.

Bob did a little bow, said, "After you"; as he swooped his arm in the direction of the door, he had just pulled open.

"Well thank you", Julia said with a smile.

"What I do best", he said as he followed her into the restaurant foyer,

The hostess was just coming back after seating some guests and Asked, "Two?"

Julia said, "Oh no. We're not together"

"Oh", the hostess said as she looked around the room to see if there were any single tables available.

"Wait here; I will see what I can find."

Bob and Julia looked at each other and shrugged their shoulders.

When the hostess returned, she said their might be a little wait for a single table.

Bob tapped Julia on the shoulder and said, "Look, if you are alone and since I am alone, maybe the hostess might be able to find a table for two faster."

"Are you sure?" Julia asked and wondering why she asked that to a perfect stranger..

"It would be my treat." Bob said.

"How can anyone refuse such an offer?" Julia said with a smile.

The relieved hostess smiled and said, "OK, follow me. Would you like a table of a booth?"

"Booth", they both said at the same time.

The hostess escorted them to a booth on the window side and put the menus on the table. "Your server will be with you shortly", she said.

Bob waited until Julia sat down and had scooted herself into the middle of the seat.

He didn't sit himself until Julia was settled.

"Nice", she was thinking.

The server came to the booth and said, "Hi Julia," She was saying that to Julia but all the time looking at Bob.

"Hi Sally", Julia said with a bit of a grin.

She knew what Sally was thinking about this guy that came in with her.

Bob looked over to Julia and asked, "You must eat here a lot."

"Yeah, sort of, but Sally and I are old friends, we go way back."

"So, what can I get you two to drink?" Sally asked.

"Water for me", Julia said.

"Is the water very wet?" Bob asked still looking down at the menu.

"Huh?" Sally asked.

"Sorry just a little bit of nervous humor" Bob answered.

With his head still down, he raised his eyes to see Julia with a puzzled look on her face.

"Oh boy", he thought.

"I'll be back to take your order", Sally said as she left while still looking back at Bob..

"So what looks good?" Bob asked

"I like the salmon", Julia said breaking her puzzled look.

Bob closed the menu and gave a puzzled look at her.

"What?" Julia asked.

Bob just kept studying her for a few moments.

Seemed like an eternity to Julia.

"I suppose we should introduce each other," he finally said leaning forward.

Julia leaned forward looking at him straight in his eyes. "I'm Julia, who the heck are you?" she asked. Then smiled.

Bob leaned back and said, "OooooKay"

Then he picked up and opened the menu again.

"I'm Bob. So you like salmon?"

"Yup," She said. Then picked up and opened her menu.

"Bob, still studying the menu, "That's one thing we have in common."

Sally returned holding up her order pad and looking at Julia, "My guess it will be the salmon?" she asked with pencil ready.

"What else?" she answered with a grin.

Then she turned to Bob. "And you, sir?"

Bob looked over at Julia and asked, "Did she just call me 'sir' pointing toward Sally with his thumb.

"OK then, I will have same thing my fiancée is having." He said with a smirk, closing the menu and handing it to Sally.

Julie's mouth dropped as well as Sally's pad and pencil.

Bob put his hands together on the table and turned back and forth to Julie and Sally with a crazy smile on his face.

Sally finally composed herself enough to pick up her pad and pencil off the floor and said to Julie, "I didn't know."

"You still don't." Julie said just looking at Bob who by now was looking out of the window. She could see a smirky smile on his face.

She finally said, "Well that's got be a first. A ten-minute romance and a marriage proposal. That is if I read you correctly."

"Humor is my middle name. It has gotten me in a lot of trouble all my life. Oh, by the way, are you married? I should have asked that first." He asked leaning forward to her.

"No. Are you?" she said first leaning back in her seat then leaning toward him.

"Nope. There's another thing we have in common." He said. Then he looked back out the window.

Julia, by this time, was trying to figure Bob out. She was wondering if he is for real.

Wanting to continue the conversation, Bob asked, "You live around here?"

"Yeah, up the street little. It's the Devonshire Apartments. I have lived there for three years."

"Sounds upscale," Bob said.

"Yeah, but sounds can be deceiving. They are just plain old apartments, but kept up nicely. There is a manager on site which makes it nice." She remarked while looking out the window.

"How about you? Do live around here? She asked looking back at Bob.

"I just moved into the Camel Back Mountain town houses up that way," as he looked around trying to figure which way to point.

"Wow, talk about upscale. I have a friend that lives there and she's a lot richer than I will ever be."

Then she pointed in the direction behind Bob. "It's that way"

"Thanks. That will help me find my way home. Where do you work?" he asked.

"I work for Warren Enterprises. It's a big conglomerate from Detroit." She answered with a little bit of pride in her voice.

"You sound like it is a good place to work." He said as he pushed back into his seat because Sally returned with their food.

"Oh it really is. We have many great people working there and the management is the best. I will probably work there my entire life. If they let me, that is," she added.

"Well, I will have to look it up if it is a great as you say," he said as he unrolled the silver ware out of his napkin and reached for his fork.

"If you are looking for work, one of my best friends works in Human Resources. I could put in a good word for you……after all, being 'engaged' and all."

They looked at each other both in deep thought.

Julia broke the trance and asked, "So how do you like your salmon?"

"I will let you know after I take my first bite." He said pulling the plate closer.

"Oops. Sorry I didn't notice you hadn't tried it yet." She said. "I was just trying to shake off the thought I was just having."

Bob looked at her, held up a finger and started to make a comment but decided to let well enough alone.

The rest of the meal went quietly with just a few comments about the great taste of everything.

Sally returned to the booth after seeing they were finished with their meal and asked if the wanted to see the desert menu.

"Gotta be kidding." Bob said rubbing his stomach. Then said, "Oops, should have asked you." He said looking at Julia.

"Oh, my gosh no." she said wiping the mouth with her napkin

"OK then." Sally said taking the bill out or her apron pocket and holding it out.

Bob immediate took it and leaned over to get his wallet out of his rear pocket.

"Wait I minute," Julia said as she opened her purse. "I want to pay my share."

"Oh no! Do you realize what my sainted mother do if I let my date pay her way? My guess she would find a way to kick me in the butt." He said as he pulled a credit card from his wallet.

"Wow. Platinum American Express. I am impressed." Sally said as she gently pulled the card out of Bob's hand with a thumb and fore finger.

"Don't look anything into that, it's just my show-off maneuver.

Julia and Bob made some idle talk while they were waiting for Sally to bring back the tab for him to sign.

Bob got up, went over to Julia and offered his hand to help her out of the booth.

That gesture and the warmth of Bob's soft hand gave a warm tender feeling to Julia.

They walked out of the restaurant, stopped and faced each other.

"It's that way," Julie said as she pointed it the direction of Bob's town house.

"Thanks. Never could have found it with out your direction." He said, looking back over his shoulder.

"Least I could do for a free dinner," she said in a coy manner.

Bob was thinking that perhaps he might reach out for a hug, but he thought that perhaps a handshake would be more appropriate.

He held out his hand, and as she took it, he placed his other hand over hers.

That warm tender feeling fell over her again.

"Perhaps we may meet again like this," he said looking deeply into her eyes.

"I would like that." It was a sincere comment.

As she turned to walk toward her car, she looked back and noticed Bob was still sanding there watching her.

Bob turned and started for his car. He stopped, put his hand up to his chin and thought, "What just happened here?"

Julia reached her car, got in, plopped her purse on the passenger seat, put both hands on the steering wheel and thought, "What just happened here?"

The next morning, Julia was talking with a few of her co-workers about the experience at the restaurant the night before.

"So when's the wedding?" one of the girls asked; noting the comment Bob made about being engaged

"Not sure, but you gals will be the first to find out." She answered thinking to herself that it would be nice. But……….maybe too soon.

Not sure why she thought that.

Just then, Anita, the office manager came in and announced that one of the Vice Presidents from Detroit would be here this morning and we all must be alert and sharp. "I believe he is also one of the brothers who own this company." She added making it sound especially important to put on a good face.

About then, a group of important looking men entered the room. Everyone immediately began to look as busy as they could.

Julia gasped. There was Bob with them.

All the office staff stood and greeted the men as Anita started to introduce each one.

"This Mary and that is Betty and she is Nancy and….where is Julia?" she asked looking around.

"There is someone hiding behind you." Bob said trying to look around her.

"Julia! What are you doing back there?" Anita asked with a puzzled look on her face.

"Hi there," Julia said as she peeked around and gave a little coy wave to Bob. "We meet again."

All the others knew exactly why Julia had been hiding behind Anita. Here obviously was the guy Julia was taking about earlier.

"Why didn't you tell me who you were last night?" Julia asked.

"Well my name being Bob Warren, and you working for Warren Enterprises, I thought you might put two and two together and come up with four or maybe have an epiphany." He said with a silly grin on his face.

"Math was never my one of my strong points. I am never going to live this down," Julia added with bowed head.

"You won't have to. I thought it was funny… Sweet as a matter of fact." Bob said trying to make her feel better.

After he left, all the girls gathered around Julia with non-stop questions. Julia just sat there with the blush still on her face.

"All right girls, lets get back to work. You can chat about that at break time," Anita said.

As Bob and the other managers were walking down the hall to the next office, Jim Perkins, the auditor asked, "What was that all about with that gal back there?"

"I met her last night and had a rather interesting evening," Bob said with a broad smile and looking straight down the hall.

"Oh?" Jim asked.

"Not what I think you may be thinking," Bob answered as he turned into the office across the hall for his next visit.

Jim Perkins smiled but wondered if perhaps there may a gal in this office for another similar surprise.

There wasn't

Julia was having a hard time working that day. She would stare off in no particular direction, shake her head and make a deep sigh.

Diane, the gal who worked next to her noticed and asked, "Seems you are still thinking about this morning"

"Yeah, I sure am," she said bowing her head. "I can't believe that I didn't catch his name, let alone match it to the company. I figured he was just another ordinary guy. Nice however," she added.

Then she dropped her head and said, "I even told him that I would help him get a job here."

"Ouch. So where do you think this will go from here? Diane asked with raised eyebrows and a smile.

"Oblivion comes to mind," Julia said as she looked down at her desk and opened up the file she was supposed to have been working on all day.

The following Monday, Julia was staring at her computer screen in deep concentration trying to figure out what keys she needed to press in order to print out the report she had just spent several days preparing. She had not received instruction for a new computer system.

A familiar voice behind her asked, "Julia, right?"

She spun around and there stood Bob with a big grin.

"Am I that hard to remember after all we have been through and your proposal?" she asked as a comeback. She reflected his grin.

"Ah yes, now I remember you," he quipped.

"Do you have any lunch plans for today?" he added.

She reached into one of her desk drawers and pulled out a brown bag lunch.

He took it from her, handed it to Diane at the next desk that had been watching all this and said, "Here, enjoy."

"Now you've done it. You will need to buy me lunch after that maneuver," Julia said while crossing her arms.

"That was the point I was trying to make," he said. "See you at noon."

"Keep up the good work everybody he said as he noticed everyone in the room had bewildered looks on their faces.

Shortly before noon, Bob walked into the office and up to Julia's desk. He was holding a rose.

Everyone in the office was saying "Aaw."

Julia looked over to Anita and said, "I'm taking my lunch hour now."

"Hour? Yeah, right," She said with a wave.

The restaurant he chose was in the next block so they just walked to it. He held out his arm, which she gladly took. They smiled at each other as they started with a skip and a hop down the sidewalk.

"I believe everyone is looking at us," Julia said turning to look back.

"They probably think we are on the yellow brick road to OZ, he said with a big grin.

"I would have suggested we go to 'our' restaurant, but it's a little bit far. Hope you don't mind this one," he said apologetically.

"Yeah. This is good. but I hear the big bosses in the 'Ivory Tower' don't want workers taking long lunch breaks." She said looking straight ahead.

"Tyrants! Besides, I know someone up there so don't you worry," he said.

The hostess sat them in a far corner booth. They checked the menu and ordered the businessman's lunch. Then they sat there staring at each other for a few minutes.

Bob was the first to talk. "OK, where, shall we start," he asked.

"Start?" she shot back.

"Yeah, I thought we might get to know each other a little better."

"OK. I will start by asking about your mother. You referred to as 'Sainted' so I am almost afraid to ….. Is she still with us?" she asked with a concerned look.

"No, sad to say both my parents went together thanks to a foggy night and an impaired driver," he said looking off in the distance.

"Oh, I am so sorry. It must be hard to talk about them," she said as she reached across the table and squeezed his hand.

Bob looked down at their hands, then back into Julia's eyes. She could see tears welling up in his eyes.

Bob went on, "I was just sixteen and still in high school, my brother Mike was half way through college and my oldest brother, Frank was already working for the family business. Fortunately, he was smart enough to take over completely. Actually, it is because of him that the business grew as large and as fast as it has. He manages the main office in Detroit, Mike runs the Denver office and I just became the manager of this Phoenix office. At least I am about to try manage it."

"Sounds like you have a couple of great siblings," she said.

"Yeah, they got the brains and the brawn and I got the clown suit," he said with a chuckle.

"What?" she asked.

"I have never been a serious type. I see, or at least try to find humor in everything," he said shrugging his shoulders. "That sometimes gets me in a whole lot of trouble."

"I surmised that at our first meeting. Actually, I think that is a fine quality in a person. I am not trying to be patronizing. I really believe that," she said reaching over with her other hand.

"Well, enough about me. How about you?" he asked and noticed Julia taking back her hands. He pulled them back.

She looked down and smiled.

"I grew up in a small town in Montana. My dad is the Police Chief and my mom was the nurse at Doctor Fremont's clinic. I loved living in a small town where it is quiet and slow." She said that with a proud expression on her face.

"Any bothers or sisters?" Bob asked.

"No, I was an only child. I was my dad's 'Princess' and he spoiled me rotten. He was something special and he instilled basic confidence in me," she said looking like she was remembering times past.

"I can see that," he said.

"And just how did you mean that? Spoiled or Princess like?" She asked with a grin.

"I think I just dug me a hole." He grinned back at her.

"Just how did you end up working for us?" he asked, changing the subject.

"I really wasn't too keen on going to college, but I didn't want to disappoint my dad and mom so I at least went to the local junior college and got an associate degree in accounting.

One of my High School friends had moved here and got a job with you. She raved about it so much that I took her up on her invitation to join her and here I am. You met her earlier. You gave her my sack lunch,"

She pretended to wipe her brow after that long narrative.

"Do you miss being back there?" he asked.

"Yeah, but I still go back for special celebrations like holidays and town functions. I was there last month on my birthday. I think half the town greeted me."

"That is so nice. Pardon me for asking, but are you or have ever been married? I believe I asked that the other night, but I wasn't paying that much attention," he said.

"No. not even close. I kept looking for someone like my dad but he set the bar pretty high so I haven't found anyone near his qualities."

Bob sat back a looked as if he was in deep thought,

"Did I say something wrong?' she said genuinely concerned.

Bob had thoughts that perhaps he and Julia might become 'item', at some point. Of course, he did not want that to come out and suggest that just yet. Sounded to him like there may be a roadblock after what she just said about her father.

On the other had, Julia was hoping that what she just said would not jeopardize any relationship she, perhaps, might like.

Only the future would tell.

Julia got back to work a little late and told Anita she was sorry.

Anita said, "I believe you probably have a number one best excuse. How did your lunch go?"

All the other girls took notice and hoping for some juicy tidbits.

Julia did not look at any one in particular and said that it was just a routine lunch.

She went straight to her desk, sat down and leaned back into her chair.

She looked content. Everyone noticed.

Bob got back to his office just as late as Julia did but no one was concerned.

Sandi Best, his secretary, seemed annoyed because she knew where, and with whom, he went to lunch with.

Sandi was a beauty, tall, always with perfect makeup and hairstyle. She always drew attention wherever she went.

Bob did not choose her. He inherited her from the previous manager and just seemed to tolerate her for what she was, or what she thought she was.

Sandi would make any excuse to enter Bob's office and show off her dimples, knees and cleavage. She was good at it.

She was disappointed that he did not seem to notice. She would try her best to change all that.

The weeks seemed to fly past with Bob being super busy getting things the way he wanted them to be.

There would be a few visits and lunches with Julia and it appeared, at least to Julia, that things were starting to look serious.

One Friday afternoon when everyone was getting ready to leave for the weekend, Bob darted into Julia's office and asked, "You know what would be fun."

"I can think of a number of things," Julia said with a grin.

"We ought to go back to that restaurant, *'our'* restaurant and pull off the same routine," he said with excitement in his voice.

"Yeah, that would be a 'Hoot'," Julia agreed. "Let's do it!"

"OK, I will meet you there a six o'clock,"

Right at the stroke of six, they met at the door.

Bob opened the door and let Julia go in first. He lagged back for effect.

"The hostess spotted them and said, "Well Hi there you *two*."

Julia turned back to Bob and said, "Oops, she's on to us,"

They all laughed as the hostess led them to the same booth they sat in that first evening.

Peggy spotted them immediately and ran over. The first thing she did was grab Julia's left hand to see if there might be a special ring or two on her third finger.

She dropped Julia's hand, turned to Bob and said, "OK funny guy, why isn't there a brand on this girl?"

Bob shook his head a little then said, almost under his breath, "working on it."

Julia gasped and wondered if what she heard really what she heard.

Bob ignored the two gals who were just standing there looking at each other.

"Wet water will be fine for me," he said, looking at Peggy with a grin. Then he stood waiting for Julia to sit.

He swooped his arm toward the booth seat and, with a bow asked, "Would madam care to be seated?"

Peggy turned and started toward the service counter to get the water. She was shaking her head and saying, "This guy's too much."

After their meal and a lot of friendly bantering back and forth between the three, Julia and Bob went out to the sidewalk and faced each other the same way they did way the first time.

Julia stuck out her hand for a shake. Bob looked down at it and asked, "you mean after I just spent a fortune feeding you, all I get is a hand shake?'

They dove into each other with a tight-tight hug. They looked into each other's eyes and almost kissed. "Perhaps another time." they were both thinking as they parted and headed to each other's cars.

That night Julia was lying in her bed looking up at the ceiling. "I wonder what Bob meant when he said, 'working on it'," she actually said it aloud.

Bob was lying in his bed at the same time and was wondering how Julia would take it if I asked her to go steady. "Boy, I sound just like a school kid. However......,"

One day, Anita was waving a file around over her head and was asking, "This file needs to go up to the '*Ivory Tower*'. "Any volunteers?" she was purposely not looking in Julia's direction.

Everyone else immediately looked at Julia.

Julia tried to make it look like a real chore, but said, "Well, I suppose if somebody has to do it, hand it over. I will make the trip."

No need to wonder what all the smiles by every one else meant.

Julia took the elevator to the third floor where all the 'honchos' worked. It was commonly known as the *'Ivory Tower'*

She had been there before so she immediately walked up to Bob's office door, started to knock then almost dropped the file.

There was Sandi with a chair pulled up close to the side of Bob's desk and appeared to be in deep conversation. She was dressed in her usual tight, short outfit and leaning forward toward Bob.

What she was trying to show left no imagination.

Julia turned quickly around and ran to the elevator. A few people noticed and wondered what made her do that.

She got back to her office, rushed to her desk, sat heavily down in her chair and pulled a Kleenex from a desk drawer.

Everyone was looking back and forth to each other and shrugging their shoulders.

Anita immediately ran to her to find out what the matter was.

Julia could not even talk at first. She looked up at Anita with tears in her eyes and asked. "Since it is almost quitting time, would you mind if l left now?"

"Of course you may. Can I do anything for you?" she asked looking concerned and shaking her head.

"No, but thank you anyway. I just want to go home and close myself in," she said as she picked up her purse and headed for the door.

All the girls gathered around Anita trying to find out what happened,

Just then, Bob came into the office and after looking around asked, "Where is Julia?"

Anita said she left a little early and told him that she seemed to be upset about something.

"Hum," Bob said, "I hope it's nothing serious."

Julia went to her apartment, closed the door and went into the bedroom where she plopped across her bed. She rolled over, grabbed her stuffed teddy bear, and started to hug it.

As she was lying there looking up at the ceiling, she was wondering to herself why she got so upset. After all, she and Bob were not really committed to each other. She was angry with herself for taking things for granted.

She finally decided that she may have assumed too much and went to the kitchen to make her a nice cup of tea.

Bob was sitting in his car in the parking garage. He had both hands on the steering wheel as he stared out the windshield. He was concerned about Julia and her sudden leaving the office.

Reaching for the starter he said, out loud," Sure hope it was nothing serious."

There was an inter-branch meeting scheduled back in Detroit and Bob was expected to be there to report progress for his branch.

Bob was having a competition race with his brother Mike from the Denver office. Both wanted to show off for their brother Frank who, of course, was the big boss over everything.

Both Frank and Mike were married with families so these meeting were always a family blast.

Of course, Bob would always be alone at all these functions, which gave his brothers teasing time. All in good fun of course.

Bob had plans to make his two brothers 'eat their words' this time. "Just wait until they get a load of Julia," he was thinking. Julia did not know it, but he was going to ask her to accompany him to Detroit. He hinted to his brothers that they would be in for a surprise.

Bob walked into Julia's office with a smile that quickly vanished after he noted all the dirty looks he was getting from every one in the room.

"Strange," he thought.

By this time, Julia had told all the other gals about what she had seen in Bob's office between him and Sandi. He was not aware of that, of course.

He stood in front of Julia's desk, smiled and waited for her to look up.

She finally did and said rather coolly, "Oh. Hello," then looked back down at her desk.

"Well what kind of a greeting is that?" he asked.

"Oh, did you need something?" she said without looking up.

"Yeah, but if you are busy, I could come back," he answered with a puzzled look on his face.

"OK. What is it?" She said as she took off her glasses and dropped them on the desk.

"I have to go to a company meeting in Detroit on Wednesday and I thought maybe you would like to go with me?"

Julia looked up, took a moment and said, "No." Then picked up her glasses and started to look busy again.

Bob stood there in shock. "Wow!" he thought. "I guess I may have missed all the signals."

"Well then, OK," he said but stood there for a few moments. Then he backed up a couple of steps and repeated, "OK."

He wished he could have crawled back out of the office so no one would see him. He tried not to look like the beaten puppy dog he felt like.

After he left, all the girls rushed to Julia's desk. She was crying.

Bob got back to his office, sat there for a while trying to figure what just happened here.

Sandi came in and noticed the dejected look of Bob's face. "You OK boss?" she asked.

"Not sure. I just have some thinking to do,' he said looking up at Sandi with a 'help me' look on his face. If he would have been looking for some comfort, Sandi would be the last person to give him any.

Sandi could not care less about his feelings. She was that kind of person.

"Oh, by the way, your formal invitation and itinerary for your Detroit trip came a few minutes ago. I noticed you have two of everything. Is someone going with you?" she asked.

"I thought so, but I guess I was wrong," he said as her reached for the pack Sandi was holding out.

"I am available." She said with a little hope in her expression.

"Thanks, Sandi. Very thoughtful of you," he said with a half smile not realizing what he just said.

"Think about it." Sandi said with a coy smile.

Bob sat at his desk for the rest of the afternoon. He would shake his head; put his hand up to his chin as if in deep thought.

I wonder why Julia was like that?" he kept murmuring to him self.

Bob was walking past Julia's office and thought he would go in to see if perhaps there might have been a reason for that last meeting.

Julia happened to look up just as Bob started in.

He gave a smile and a little wave.

She immediately looked down.

That stopped him in is tracks. He backed out, dropped his head and started down the hall.

Anita noticed that and went over to Julia's desk.

Julia was crying.

As Bob walked past Sandi's desk, he said, with out looking at her, "Get packed."

Sandi put both fists up under her chin, looked up toward heaven and said, "YES!"

Sandi and Bob were on an airplane on their way to Detroit.

Bob was quiet most of the way but Sandi was a chatterbox. She told him her life story including being a cheerleader and prom queen in high school and a modeling gig when she was in college.

He listened politely but when he would look at her he was wishing that Julia would be the one sitting there.

When they landed in Detroit, a limo driver greeted them and showed them to the vehicle that he had parked in one of the VIP parking spaces.

"I could really go for this," Sandi was thinking.

The driver drove them to the company office tower in near downtown where he escorted them to the third floor large meeting room.

It was crowded with employees and guests enjoying the pre-meeting gathering.

Bob and Sandi walked up behind brothers Frank and Mike.

He tapped them on the shoulders and said, "I would like you to meet Sandi,"

They both turned around and Frank said, "Wow!" the held out his had to Sandi.

Mike gasped and almost dropped his glass. Every body noticed.

Mike grabbed Bob's arm and led him to a near corner.

"What?" Bob asked with a frown.

"What hell is SHE doing here?" he asked matching Bob's frown.

"She works more me, or rather us. Do you know her?" he tried to explain.

"Oh yeah, I knew her when I was interning in Phoenix, and I can tell you, every guy *knew* her back then. Check it out for yourself when you get back.

"Oooh boy, wish I had known that," Bob said looking back at Sandi who seemed to be flirting with every man near her.

Bob spent the evening wondering how he got himself into this. All he could think about if only he knew what was wrong with Julia, perhaps this could have been a much more enjoyable visit.

When the party was over, Frank, his wife and kids and Mike and his wife and son along with Bob and Sandi were all taken by limo to the family estate in the suburbs.

They spent a few hours reminiscing about times gone by. There was a lot of teasing directed toward Bob since he was the 'baby' in the family.

Thelma, the long time maid and the nana to Bob his whole life, was in her glory, Here were all 'her boys' back together in one place. It was also sad for her because the senior Warrens were not there to enjoy these moments.

She would just sit among everyone and have long bouts of memory-filled moments.

For some reason, she could not find it in her heart to accept Sandi for Bob. She really did not know why. She just felt Bob deserved better. Oh well, his choice she thought. She would accept it.

The evening grew to a close and everyone was heading off to the bedrooms.

Thelma's ears perked up when she heard Sandi ask Bob where *their* bedroom was.

"Well, mine is my old room over there in the west wing as he pointed in that direction and yours will be where ever Thelma has made up a guest suite for you." He pointed it the opposite direction.

Thelma got a wide grin on her face. What was going through in her mind was which guest suite was the farthest end of the east wing

The company and board meetings lasted for three days. While the men toiled in all those meetings, the ladies would go out shopping. The men did not object.

Bob gave Sandi one of his credit cards so she would not seem left out.

Frank and Mike's wives would cringe when they noticed that Sandi felt that she could buy as she pleased. They would look at each other and shake their heads. They were sure that Bob would be in for a shock when he got his next monthly credit card statement.

The meetings were finally over and everyone headed to the estate for one last get-together.

This was Frank's home but Mike and Bob would be heading off back to Denver and Phoenix.

Mike and his wife and son would be leaving on the early flight and Bob and Sandi would be on a mid afternoon flight.

The morning seemed to come too fast. Everyone was sitting at the huge table in the big country kitchen enjoying the breakfast that Thelma had prepared.

The limo arrived for Mike and his gang so they all went out with him for some last hugs.

Bob was feeling uncomfortable seeing Sandi there trying to be so familiar with everyone as if she was part of the family.

Bob helped Thelma do the kitchen clean up while Sandi wandered around the house with the idea that maybe some day…..well.

When it got close to Bob and Sandi's time to leave, Thelma cornered Bob wanting to say special good byes.

She was a tiny lady so Bob would prick her up for their hugs. When he lifted her down, she backed up a bit and looked deeply at Bob.

He asked, "What is it Nana?"

Thelma said, "Don't……just be careful. Be very care full," she pleated

"Of what, Nana?" he asked with a worried look on his face.

Thelma looked in Sandi's direction.

"Oh, Nana. Believe me, she is just a fill in so to speak. The gal I really love and want to be with is back in Phoenix. You will love her, I am sure," he assured her.

"So then why is *she* here?" Thelma asked again looking in Sandi's direction.

"It's a long story. One in which I aim to correct when I get back," he said with a head nod.

That seemed to satisfy Thelma.

Bob and Sandi got to the airport and checked in their luggage. Bob wondered how Sandi ended up with three suitcases. He was almost certain she only had two on the flight from Phoenix. He was about find out when his credit card statement would come later in the month.

Bob was determined to find out why Julia was bushing him off. He went down to her office, walked up to her desk looked her straight in the eyes and said, "We need to talk."

"Is it about a girl named Sandi?" She asked, "I hear you two went on a trip last week. That is all everybody has been talking about."

His shoulders dropped he shook his head and said, "That was supposed to be you, not Sandi but your never seemed interested. The last day you gave me the cold shoulder, I was so upset, I asked the first available gal I Saw," he tried to explain. Then added, "It was the worst mistake I could have made. Just ask my brothers and my Nana."

She looked puzzled, leaned back into her chair and said, "I don't understand. From what I was seeing about the two of you, it certainly looked like a couple to me," she stopped for a minute and added, "Your Nana?"

"Where did you get the idea that Sandi and I had anything going?" he demanded.

"I saw you sitting extremely close together in your office one day. She was all over you," Julia said as she crossed her arms and leaning back in a defiant way.

"Wow. I cannot visualize that picture. It is a real *yuck* vision in my mind. Believer me, that could not be more wrong! I'm so sorry you think that it was what it could be," It was a genuine concern he was feeling.

Julia took a long deep look at Bob.

"Is there any way we can turn this into something funny?" She reached over and took both Bob's hands giving them a little squeeze.

He gave her a wide grin and said, "You missed one heck of a trip."

"Your Nana?" she asked with a little giggle.

Bob got back to his office relieved and going though his mind, that he and Julia could do to celebrate the moment.

He walked past Sandi without even looking at her and the mail and messages she was holding up for him. She followed him and went up to the side bar of his desk.

He noticed her standing there holding up the notes and mail for him to take. He noticed how close she could stand next to the side bar.

He looked at her, then down at the side bar of his desk and suddenly realized that Sandi would always pull up 'close' to him.

"Aha," he thought and made a mental note to have this desk replaced with one that does not have a side bar. It would not hurt to add a cage. He was even picturing a moat around it.

Sandi was wondering why Bob was smiling.

Sandi could not wait to brag about her trip to Detroit. She would tell every one who would listen about the first class flight and all the limo rides to where ever she wished to go. She especially described about the stay at the family estate and all the servants that catered her needs. She went into great detail about the shopping trips with Bob's sisters in law. She made it sound perhaps, she would be a permanent part of this family one day..

Most took it as a 'grain of salt' as the saying goes. However, they wondered why Bob fell for it. They all knew Sandi and could not picture the two of them as a couple.

Bob was in a dilemma. He knew he had to come up with some way to distance himself from Sandi but knew it would look bad for both of them if he just fired her.

He got in touch with Vera, his human resources manager, to see what the best approach might be.

The first thing Vera said was, "I wondered how long it would have taken you to get rid of her. There is a pool on the bulletin board down in our office with number of weeks listed. I have week six. Do not worry; we will take care of it for you.

Do mind if I wait until after the 20th. That would be the sixth week.

Bob just shook his head, smiled. He then nodded his approval.

A better reason came with his credit card statement.

Sandi tried so cover the amount when she was getting him to approve it. However, he got a glance, which made him gasp. That third suitcase on the return flight from Detroit now made sense to him.

Sandi was now a former employee of the Warren Company.

Julia was deep in thought at her desk. She was trying to come up with a solution to a project problem Anita had given her.

She glanced up and saw a smiling Bob headed in her direction.

She sighed, moved her computer mouse to the side, dropped her glasses on her desk and shot a similar smile back at him.

"Gotta choice," he said as he approached, "Lunch today or back to 'our' restaurant tonight?"

"Any chance we could do both?" she asked jokingly.

"Not that hungry, but your every wish is my command," he replied.

"We haven seen Sally for awhile," she hinted.

"Pick you up at six. We could do our usual entry, but I think we might over do it," he said with a smile and a nod, "They are on to us anyway."

Apparently, Julia and Bob became rather popular at the restaurant. When they entered, there were cheers from all corners.

Of course, there were some diners who didn't know what all the fuss was about, but soon got to know them as a cute couple.

After their meal, they found themselves standing in the familiar spot just out side of the entrance.

They stood looking at each other. After a moment of silence Bob asked, "Your place or mine?" Then quickly put his hands over his mouth.

Julie stepped back and had a shocked look on her face. "Do I understand exactly what you meant by that question?" she asked.

"Probably not. I'm sorry I asked that….sort of," he answered. "Sorry I asked."

"Oh, that's OK. I got the message, but please understand I'm really not ready just yet," she said in a sincere manner.

"You just made me respect and love you even more, if that is at all possible."

"I have told you that I love you, have I not?" he asked with a expression of wonder.

"You have said that in more ways that you could possibly imagine," she said as she gave hin a hug and a kiss on the cheek; turned and headed to her car

That left Bob standing there scratching his head.

"What just happened here?" he wondered as he headed for his car.

The next morning he stopped by Julia's office before he went to his. He took her by the arm and led her out into the hallway.

He looked both ways to make sure no one could hear him.

"You're not a Nun or something, are you?" as he looked into her eyes.

"Got you a little confused last night, did I?" she asked with a chuckle.

"No, I just wanted to make sure you are what I had hoped you would be. I could not be happier. I love you Julia," he said as he turned and started down the hall.

Julia stood there slightly shaking her head and thinking, "This is turning into and unbelievable romance."

Anita, who had been standing behind her said, "Shall we go in?"

Julia jumped and turned around to see Anita with a knowing grin on her face.

"You don't have to say anything," Anita said. I am so happy for you."

It was a busy time for the company. New products had been advertised which caught the Phoenix manufacturing and shipping departments off guard.

Bob and most of the senior staff found themselves working many long hours.

That meant time away from Julia.

They had a meeting in one of the conference rooms and it was agreed that Bob would go to the Denver office or back to the Detroit facility to see if they might be able to give a hand in helping to fulfill at least some of the orders.

He told one of the guys in the meeting to go down to engineering and have them give you the drawings and specification. Also any models they have available.

"Oh, and while you're at it, would you mind having Donna, my new secretary, make travel arrangements.

Two reservations," he instructed.

They all looked and smiled to each other. Julie was about to go on a trip.

The next morning, he was standing in front of Julia's desk.

"I will be leaving on Wednesday for a trip back to Detroit," he announced as he held up a trip ticket jacket.

"Well I don't think I have to worry about Sandi going with you this time," she said with an air of confidence.

Bob opened up the ticket jacket and pulled two tickets out. He handed one Julia. "I can't read the name on this ticket," he said, "Can you make it out?"

She turned the ticket over and said, "Looks like it is for someone named Julia," then she handed it back to him.

He just stood there, then put the ticked back into the jacket and started to leave.

He stopped after about three steps and asked while still facing away, "Aren't you going to say anything?"

"I don't know, why don't you check with that Julia person?"

He came back to her desk shaking his head, "You are so funny."

"I wonder where I get that?" she teased.

"Be packed and ready to go by nine AM on Wednesday," he instructed.

"YES SIR!" she gave with a smart salute.

Julia was, as expected, very excited. Mostly because she would get to know at least one of Bob's brothers, and especially the Nana.

She spent that evening taking inventory of her wardrobe and making a list of clothes she might need to supplement.

Looking in one of her drawers, she spotted a black sortie nightie. It had been a gag gift from one of her friends at a birthday party. She held it up and examined it then said, "Naw," and tossed it back.

She went back to the bed where she had everything sorted out and noticed the modest PJs. She thought about if for a while then went back to the drawer.

The black shortie nightie was about to make a trip to Detroit. "Why not," she said out loud.

Right as scheduled, Bob pulled up to Julie's apartment building in an airport taxi. Next stop: Sky Harbor Airport.

Julie had not flown much so this was a real experience for her. First Class made it an even greater experience.

When they arrived at the Detroit Metro Airport, the same limo driver who had picked up Sandi and Bob a few weeks ago greeted them.

The driver was surprised when Julia instead of Sandi stepped forward. He studied her closely then gave Bob thumbs up.

Bob smiled.

They went directly to Frank's office when they got to the building.

"Wow, you must have had a tail wind. It sure didn't take you long to get here.

"Just excited to see you Bro," Bob said as the two went into a tight embrace.

Bob stepped back, pulled Julia by the arm over to Frank and said," I would like you to meet Julia," he said.

"Well now, this is more like it. You had us all worried about that last one," he said as he pulled Julia into a hug.

"Thought you'd like that," Bob said.

Wait until Helen and the kids get to meet her," Frank said with his eyes still on Julia.

"Tonight, I hope," Bob wished.

"All set up," Frank said, continuing to look at Julia. "Ya done good little brother," then he added, "It's mid afternoon, why don't head out to the slums."

They all piled into the limo for the half hour or so drive to the "slums"

"Julie couldn't believe it when they arrived. To her it was like a movie scene and she was about to meet some Royalty.

Bob noticed her gawk and said, "Actually, it's kinda drafty."

When they pulled up to the entrance, two small boys came running up to Frank, practically knocking him over. "Easy guy, I don't need another broken arm," Frank yelled as he tried to dodge them.

"Broken arm?" Bob asked.

"Long story, tell you later," he answered as he was being chased down the drive.

"Helen came out of the door and yelled to her two boys, "Hey get back here and let your father alone." She was laughing.

She walked up to Julia who was getting out of the limo. "You're Julia, aren't you?"

"Yes I am. I am surprised that you knew my name," she smiled.

"You would be surprised what we know about you. For instance, we understand Bob introduced you as his fiancée to the server at a restaurant the first time you met."

Julia looked over at Bob who was getting out of the other side of the limo.

He just shrugged his shoulders.

Just then, a tiny elderly lady came out of the door.

Julia spotted her and said, "You have just got to be Nana," said as she rushed over to greet her.

Thelma (Nana) yelled over to Bob and demanded, "Get over here!"

Bob, with all smiles grabbed her and practically threw her into the air, "How's my best girl?" he asked and kissed her smack on the mouth.

He sat her down next to Julia and asked, "Well, what to you think?" as he directed her attention to Julia.

Thelma studied Julia and asked, "Is this the best you could find as my replacement?"

Julia did not know what to say. She thought it must be some joke. It was.

Thelma pulled Julie down closer to her size, gave her a tight hug and said, "You are everything Bobby said you were."

"Bobby? Julia asked looking and laughing at Bob.

"Nana, look at me, I'm all grown up," he scolded her.

Thelma turned to Julia and said, "He will always be Bobby to me." Julia was grinning.

"Oh boy," Bob, alias Bobby, was thinking,

Why are we all standing out here? Let's go in and get these two settled," Frank said as he grabbed the handles of the suitcase and headed for the door.

Julia came to a dead stop when she entered the great room. She looked up and around at everything. "Unbelievable," she was murmuring.

Bob walked passed her and whispered out of the side of his mouth, "Drafty."

Bob called Thelma over and asked what room she had for Julia.

"Silly boy," she said with a wink.

"Oh wait Nana, we had better think about that. Not to sure that Julia would approve.

"Gotta be kidding," three voices said that at the same time.

Four, if you count the quiet comment that came from Julia.

"Well I *would* like to see where you spent your youth," Julia said in a coy manner.

After the special dinner that Nana Thelma prepared, they all went into the parlor for coffee and a dessert pie.

Most of the evening's conversation was at Bob's expense. Frank and Nana were telling stories; mostly about Bob's funny and embarrassing moments

Bob spent most of time denying or trying to explain them.

Julia was taking it all in with special attention.

Later, Frank mouthed, "look," as he pointed to Nana. She was sound asleep.

"Looks like a signal," Frank said.

Just then, Nana woke up and looked around, "Sorry, I must have dozed off. What did I miss?" she asked in a groggy voice.

"Just my life from age twelve through fourteen," Bob said.

"Oh, that's was the best part," Nana said.

"We're heading for the sack, Nana," Frank said.

"Bob got up, held out his hand to Julia and asked, "Shall we?"

Julia took his hand and gave a silent "yes"

He kept holding her hand as they walked down the hall to the staircase and up to the second floor and Bob's bedroom.

The six eyes from those still in the parlor were following them.

They walked down the hall in silence until they came to Bob's bedroom door.

He opened it, reached around and turned on the light switch.

He swooped his arm toward the opening and said, "After you."

Julia went in, stopped to look at all the walls that had pendants and pictures plastered on them.

"Just as I expected it would be. You must have been quite an athletic," she said as she noted the jacket hanging on wall with the big varsity letter 'P' on it and at all pictures of Bob posed as a football and basketball player.

"Not really, I was just another guy on the team," he said in a matter of fact manner tone.

Never mind that he had scored the winning touch down in a championship game or that he sunk the winning free throw that beat the school's fierce rival.

Julia took a long look at the bed that Nana Thelma had turned down earlier.

Bob pointed to a door across the room and said, "You can change in there."

Julia went over to one of the dressers where Nana Thelma had placed her suitcase. She opened it and looked at the nightclothes she had packed. She first reached for the black shortie nightie, but quickly picked up the modest PJs instead.

She smiled at Bob, held up the PJs to show him and went into the bathroom.

When she came out, Bob noticed a slight blush on her face as she headed toward the bed. "Which side?" she asked.

"Your choice," he replied, "I'm a little new at this."

Julia walked around to one side and said, "This will do nicely," as she looked at Bob for his approval.

"Good choice. Closest to the door," he said with a grin.

Julia hadn't thought about that but…..

"I will be with you in a sec," he said as he started for bathroom door.

Julia stood there next to the bed in deep thought. "What am I doing?" she was thinking.

Bob came out noticed that she was still just standing.

"Don't need an engraved invitation," he said as he pointed to the bed.

Julia pulled back the covers, slipped under them and pulled them up under her chin.

Bob just chuckled and did the same on his side.

They turned to face each other and started to laugh

In the morning, Julia woke up and slowly opened her eyes. Yes, she was still there in Bob's bedroom and in Bob's bed.

She turned over and there was Bob propped up on one elbow just looking at her with a genuine look of love in his eyes.

"Oh, good morning," she said.

"Same back at ya," he said with a wide smile.

"Did you sleep well?"

"I must have, I see its light out already," she said looking toward the window.

There was a long silence.

"Sorry about last night," she said still looking out the window.

"Don't worry about it. I felt the same way. We have a lifetime of intimacy to look forward to when you are ready. We didn't need it last night." he assured her.

It took a moment, but the "*lifetime of intimacy*' spoke volumes to Julia.

"I love you," Bob said and he reached over and gave a tender kiss.

When Julia and Bob came down to the kitchen, the table was overflowing with just about every breakfast goodies you could imagine.

Frank was sitting at the table with a wide grin on his face. "Thought you two might need some extra nourishment this morning," he said, "Helen and the boys have already eaten."

Julia and Bob just looked at each other. "If he only knew," they were both thinking.

Bob gave Julia a wink.

The meetings with Frank and Bob lasted several days. Mike, Barbara and boys had flown in from Detroit to see if there might be anything he and his facility could do to help with the problem.

There was not, but at least it got the three brothers and families together. The addition of Julia as part of that family was especially rewarding.

During the day, the sister's in law, including the future sister in law, spent most of their time going to department stores and dress shops.

Frank and Mike's wives assumed that Bob had given Julia one of his credit cards for that purpose just as he had done for Sandi.

Had they paid attention, they would have noticed Julia's name was on the cards she presented.

With all the business finished, the whole family gathered at the family estate for one last visit.

Helen, Julia, Mike's wife, Barbara along with Nana Thelma were in the kitchen doing the clean up from the meal.

All the guys were in the family room playing pool and reminiscing old times. Frank and Mike apologized to Bob for all the teasing they gave him if front Julia

He, of course, told them that it was no problem and that Julia needed to know what she is getting into. "My problem is Nana calling me 'Bobby'. I'm afraid that is going to haunt me for the rest of my life with Julia." He was kidding, or so he thought.

The ladies came in and took seats with their mates and got kisses from them all.

Julia sat as close as she could to Bob, held and squeezed his hand, He looked up at her with a, "What was that for?" look. She smiled and kissed him again.

If he could read her mind, he would see that she was thinking that this may have been all a dream to her and that she would wake up eventually. Not so, of course.

The only person in the room that felt deep sadness was Nana Thelma. For all she knew, this might very well the last time she would see her 'boys' together at one place.

She was well into her eighties and she was aware of her fate,

Two limos were parked in the front drive waiting for Mike and family and Julia and Bob's rides to the airport.

Everyone was there giving hugs and kisses.

"So, what to you think?" Bob asked as Julia sat quietly seated in the first class lounge, waiting for their flight.

She did a quick head shake as if to come our of a trance.

"Oops, did I wake you?" Bob asked.

"Well, if I am dreaming, please don't wake me 'till the rooster crows," She said looking straight at him.

"Where did that come from?" Bob asked with a puzzled look.

"I haven't the slightest idea," Julia answered scratching her head. Then added, "Oh Bob, I feel so lucky. Things like this just does not happen to a girl like me."

"I don't know why you feel that way. Boy meets girl; boy falls in love with girl; they find out all about each other and see that they belong to each other then go on to the next step.

"Simple as that," he said. Then he then said to himself, "That was pretty good, if I don't say so myself."

"Oh, thank you.....Bobby," she said with a chuckle.

"I'm gonna get that Nana," Bob said aloud.

They both laughed.

The long wait for Julia's co-workers was over and the anticipated return of Julia was finally here.

She casually walked into the office on Monday morning amid cheers and applauds.

"What's happening?" she asked as she looked around.

Anita said, "OK, let's have it."

"Have what? Did you all expect souvenirs?" she asked with a smirk on her face.

Anita and three girls were at Julia's desk all talking and asking at the same time.

"You wouldn't believe it if I told you. There is a whole different world out there and I lived in it for awhile."

She went on to describe everything from the first class flights to the limo rides and especially the Warren family estate in suburban Detroit as well as the shopping trips with Bob's brother's wives.

Anita said, "That doesn't surprise me one bit. So how do you fit into all this? Or should I not ask?"

"Oh, Anita, If I am living in a dream, I hope I never wake up," she said dropping her head.

Just then, Bob walked into the office.

Everyone first looked at him, then back to Julia then back to Bob.

"OK ladies, what has she been telling you? And if any one of you call me Bobby, I'm gonna kill her. Or at least wound her," he said trying to sound stern.

They all turned back to Julia and started laughing.

Hi kitten," Bob said as he got up to Julia's desk and brushed her cheek.

All the girls said "Kitten?" at the same time.

"How about lunch today?" he asked.

"How can I refuse such an offer from a gentleman?" she asked.

"OK, see you at noon," he said as he turned to leave.

He was certain he heard a soft, "Bye Bobby"

Julia's birthday was coming up soon and Bob wanted it to be something special for her. He knew she usually went home for the celebration and did not want to upset tradition.

When he talked about it to her, he asked how she felt if her parents and perhaps some of her friends could come here. He would be glad to host a party.

"Mom and Dad might like that. They have only been her to see me a couple of times. I am sure that they would take the time. As for others, I can't think of anyone in particular except half of the town," she said.

He remembered her telling him about small town living.

"Then do you mind if I start the ball rolling?" he asked.

"That would be nice, but sounds like a lot of work," she said looking concerned.

"I'll get help. I just need some addresses and exactly how I should address your parents," he wanted to know.

"It would probably be too soon to call them Mom and Dad." Then she put her had over her mouth realizing what she had just said. Was she assuming too much?

"let's go formal at first. I will call them Mr. Montgomery and Mrs. Montgomery. Or Sir and Madam, if you prefer," he said as he was leaving. There was a big smile on his face.

Julia hid her face with both hands and kept saying, "Stupid, stupid, stupid!"

Bob had Julia contact her parents to tell them of the plans and that Bob would be making all the arrangements for their trip here.

She had been filling them in on her life here and her relationship with Bob. They were both happy for her. At first, they were concerned because it looked like things were going too fast and they did not know anything about this 'Bob'.

From what she was telling them it sounded almost too good to be true. They were soon to find out their concerns were unfounded.

A limo driver was standing near the baggage claim carrousel at the Southwest Airlines terminal. He was holding up a sign that read: "Montgomery".

When Katherine and Roy Montgomery spotted it, they were impressed.

"That's us!" Roy yelled waving to the driver.

He came over to them and said their ride is waiting outside and that Mr. Warren had arranged to have your luggage sent directly to the Biltmore where they will be staying.

They looked at each other and shrugged their shoulders.

They were escorted to the waiting area of the VIP parking garage where the driver told them to wait there until he brought the car around.

He pulled up, got out and escorted Katherine to the car door and held it open for her. Roy had walked around and opened the door himself. The driver gave him a wave and a smile.

The drive to the Biltmore was not very long but it gave Roy and Katherine time to see some of the sites of downtown Phoenix.

Roy leaned forward and asked the driver, "This Biltmore place, is it a nice?"

"Most people seem to think so but you can judge for yourself," he said as he drove into the circle drive and up under the Porta Cochere where a gloved doorman was there to great them.

The two looked at each other with raised eyebrows and wide eyes.

The cell phone that was lying on Julia's desk was chirping and the caller ID showed a picture of her mother.

"Hi mom, did you just get in?" she asked happily.

"We sure did and we are at a place called the Biltmore," she answered.

"I know. Bob said that is where you would be staying. How to you like it? She said.

"Oh it is nice, but it must cost more that we can afford," she said in a worried voice.

"Don't worry. It is to be Bob's treat," she assured her.

"We can't ask him to pay our way," she said.

"Mom, I know you hate having things given to you, especially something grand or expensive, but believe me, there is no problem. Honest," she assured.

"Well I am sure your Dad will take it up with Bob when we meet him. When will that be, by the way?" she asked.

"Tonight, just wait for our call.

"We will be looking forward to it," her mom said, "Wanna say Hi to you dad?"

"Of course, put him on," she sounded excited.

"Hi Princess,' a familiar voice came to her over the phone.

"Hi Daddy. Did you have a nice flight?

"Yeah, but my arms are a bit tired. They started to cramp up somewhere over Flagstaff, so just soared the rest of the way in," he said trying to be funny.

"Oh, funny Daddy," she said with a laugh,

Then she suddenly realized that both her Dad and Bob were really funny guys. Maybe what I have been looking for my whole life; someone who could match my dad, was……."

"See you two tonight," she said as she pushed the 'end call' icon on her phone.

She pushed back into her chair; put a hand up to her chin and thought," This is unbelievable….but wonderful"

Bob and Julia pulled up to the Biltmore and there were her parents outside waiting for them.

"Wow, look at that," he said as he pulled up close to where they were standing.

"Just like my prompt parents,' she said with a little pride in her voice.

"Bob got out of the car and opened the door first for Julia's mom, but, before he could do the same for her father, he had already opened the door on the other side for himself.

Bob got in the driver's seat, turned to face the back seat, and said, "Hi, I'm Bob, nobody important."

He held out his hand to Julia's dad who took it and gave it a firm handshake.

"And I am Roy and this is Julie's mom, Katherine," he said.

"Hi Mrs. Montgomery," he said with a broad smile.

"Please, it's Katherine or Kate, if you prefer," she said returning the smile.

"If anyone is interested, I'm Julia," Julia said, Everyone laughed.

Bob pulled up to a familiar restaurant.

They got out of the car and Julia told her parents to wait here on the sidewalk while Bob and I go in for our routine entrance.

Roy and Katherine looked at each other but did as they had been told.

A few minutes later, they could hear a loud cheer from inside.

Julia came out all smiles and escorted them inside where Peggy greeted them and sat them down in the familiar booth.

"What's this all about?" Roy asked.

"Just our thing, daddy, this is where Bob and I met. It has become rather special to us.

"What were all the cheers we heard? You two some sore of celebrities?" Katherine asked.

Peggy answered that: "They are the cutest couple. We all love them."

"No surprise there," Roy said.

After their meal, Bob took them to his townhouse a few blocks away.

"Is this where both of you live?" Roy asked noting that it was rather upscale.

"No Daddy, I live it the other direction. My place is much smaller and not near as nice.

However, it works well for me. I'm happy with it,' she answered.

Katherine looked around at all the ambiance and said, "You must have a nice job."

Bob looked at Julia then back at Katherine and said, "Yeah, I've been lucky."

Then added, "Julia hasn't told you much about me, has she?"

Just that she thought you were special and that she was very fond of you." Katherine said acting like she wanted to know more.

Bob looked back at Julia and said, "Aw, that's nice."

Then Roy broke in and said, "She also said you treat her very nicely."

"Well sir, he told me that you are a Chief of Police, and that put the fear of God in me," he said trying to make it sound serious.

That's OK. I don't bite, and I left my handcuffs back home" he assured him

That got a laugh from everybody.

Up to this point, all that Bob had planed for was having her parents here for the celebration. As far as a party goes, he hadn't a clue.

That was solved when Anita cornered him and said that Julia was having a birthday and the girls wanted to do something special for her.

He said that he knew about the birthday but didn't know how to make a special celebration for it.

He then reached out and gave a surprised Helen a big hug. He told her that her parents are in town for her birthday.

Then he told her that she had a 'blank check' and to go for it in a big way. He also said that they could use the conference room.

"Oh thanks, Can't wait to tell the girls," she said as she tuned and practically ran down the hall back to her office.

"Whew," Bob thought, "I sure lucked out on that one."

The conference room was all-abuzz with Anita and the gals hanging decorations on all the walls and had a giant 'HAPPY BIRTHDAY' balloon hanging in the center.

Anita called Bob to come down to see if it would meet with his approval.

When he entered the room, he noticed all the ladies standing with wide smiles on their faces.

Then he noticed their handiwork and his eyes widened as he walked around the room looking at all the decorations on each wall

"Wow. This is amazing! You ladies sure went all out. This is fanatic!"

"Don't be too appreciative until you have to approve the credit card charges," Helen said with a wide grin. Although she was certain Bob would have no objection.

Bob did not respond to that because he was so entranced with all the decorations.

"Thank you all so much. This will be just great and I am sure everyone will be as thrilled as I am," Bob said still looking again at each wall and nodding his head.

The big day came and the only thing that would have make more special if it could have been a surprise party. Of course, Julia was well aware.

As expected, all the guests were awed with all the decorations.

At the head table was a giant birthday cake. Bob thought, "Wow, I hadn't even thought about that."

In his mind, he thanked Anita and the gals and would make sure he would think of some special way to repay them.

The rest of the afternoon and into the evening, everybody was mingling around wearing their silly hats and playing with their noisemakers. One would have though it was a News Years eve party.

After everyone had left Bob, Julia and her parents sat at a table. They were partially exhausted but happy.

Katherine and Roy tried to thank Bob for the party and especially for making their daughter as happy as she seemed to be.

Katherine put her hand on Bobs and told him that she could not imagine anyone would be so good and kind to Julia.

"Where did you ever come from?" she asked.

"At the neighborhood restaurant, I was on the menu," he said with a smile.

"Huh," both Katherine and Roy said together.
Bob looked over at Julia and winked.

Donna, Bob's new secretary, was running down the hall trying to catch him. She yelling, "Mr. Warren, Mr. Warren."

Bob stopped, turned back toward her and asked, "What is it?"

"You brother, Frank has been trying to reach you. It sounded important," she answered a bit out of breath..

Bob reached into his pocket for cell phone and noted that he had not turned it on this morning.

He pulled up Frank's number and tapped the call icon.

When Frank answered, the first thing he said, "Where the heck have you been?

That startled Bob because that was not like Frank to be so blunt.

Before Bob could answer, Frank said, "Never mind. It's Nana Thelma, she's in the hospital."

Bob stopped dead in his tracks and asked, "What happened? Is she OK? When did this happen? How bad is it?" he rambled on with endless questions.

Frank said that she had collapsed and right now she is in ICU and it did not look good. Then he went on to say, "I have arranged for a private jet to bring you back as soon as possible."

"Give me details," Bob demanded..

"Go out to the Scottsdale Air Park as soon as you can. There will be a jet waiting and they will fly you up to Denver to pick up Mike and Barbara." Then he added, "Bring Julia as well."

That part, Frank not needs to add.

The way Bob ran into Julia's office made everyone take notice.

He told Julia what it was all about and that they needed to make a quick trip back to Detroit

Julia looked over to Anita who was waving her hand toward the door and saying, "Go, go, go."

A half hour later, Bob and Julia were running across the tarmac at Scottsdale Air Park toward a waiting jet. One of the crew helped them board.

They were barely on board when the jet started to move toward the runway and heading for Denver.

Mike and Barbara's taxi had been parked and waiting on the tarmac at Denver; then quickly pulled up close to the jet as it came to a stop.

Helen first entered followed by Mike. Everybody gave silent, sober hugs.

The conversations during the flight were mostly about memories of the many years with Nana Thelma. There were many tender remembrances.

The jet landed at a satellite airport nearest the hospital and only took fifteen minutes to get there.

They were ushered into a room in the ICU where Frank and Helen were already sitting with sober expressions.

Nana Thelma was laying in the bed, looking peaceful. She was connected to a multitude of monitors that were measuring all her vitals. The heart monitor was making beeping sounds that matched her heartbeats.

Bob waked close to one side of the bed and held Nana Thelma's hand. Everybody noticed a slight smile starting on her face.

Mike asked Frank, "Does Nana Thelma have any family? It never occurred to ask her before," he said with a concerned look on his face.

"She had a sister but they parted a long time ago. I believe her sister had moved to Canada, but that is all I know," he said as he looked over the Bob thinking perhaps he might know since they were so close.

Bob just shrugged his shoulders.

"I called a head hunter to see what they might find. All I could do," he said looking down at Nana Thelma.

Just then, a nurse came into the room and said, "This lady says she's the patient's sister."

In walked an exact duplicate of Nana Thelma; size and all. The only difference was a slightly different hairstyle.

She said, "Hi, my mane is Velma."

She looked at her sister in the bed and then at six people with total surprised looks on their faces.

She went to the side of the bed and kissed Thelma on the forehead.

It was as if this was the moment that Nana Thelma was waiting for. The heart monitor went into constant beep.

It was over.

Later in one of the waiting rooms they were all gathered and trying to understand what had just happened here.

Frank told Velma, "I gotta tell you, Velma, you could never deny that you and Thelma are sisters."

"Just might be because we were twins," she said with a wide smile.

Frank went on, "I and Both my brothers have to apologize for not knowing about you. Our parents probably knew, but not us. I understand you live in Canada.

"That's right. I married a lumberjack forty years ago, moved to the North Country and kinda lost track of Thelma," she explained.

"Do you have any other family?" Mike broke in.

"No, we were the only kids in our family. We lost our parents a long, long time ago. And, no, I have no family and right now, I lost my Sam five years ago and I am feeling dreadfully alone.

Frank looked at Mike and Bob who were looking back at him.

"Velma, we need to talk." He said as he held out his hand.

"Call me Bobby," Bob said as he went to her and taking her other hand.

Mike also walked over to her.

All three were looking at her and for some reason, they all felt that Velma could very well become "Nana Velma".

The wives and Julia had tears running down their cheeks.

The boys arranged for Nana Thelma's final journey with the help and approval of Velma.

Nana Thelma's remains were cremated and placed in a beautiful urn.

It would forever remain somewhere at the family estate.

Mike and Bob returned to their homes with heavy hearts, but knowing that Nana Thelma was going to be replaced by Nana Velma.

Things returned to normal with Julia and Bob becoming closer and closer.

One day, Bob was standing in line at the food court in the local shopping mall. He was waiting for Julia to join him for some shopping..

Just as his coffee was handed to him, a familiar voice behind him made the hair on the back of his neck stand up.

He turned and there stood Sandi.

"Hi Ex-boss," she said as sarcastically as possible.

"Sandi! How are you?" he asked a little nervously/.

"And just how would you expect me to be?" she teased.

Bob could not come up with anything but, "Sorry. Have nice day."

The then hurried to a table.

Sandi followed him and sat down next to him.

Bob was at a complete loss for words. All he could say was that he was sorry.

Sandi wanted an explanation for her dismissal.

All Bob could think of was that third suit case and a fat credit card bill.

He was too polite to bring that up, so he didn't say anything.

"Oh, but we had so much going for us," Sandy said, reaching for his hand.

Just the Julia came around the corner to witness Sandi's maneuver.

That stopped her in her tracks. She dropped her arms and said, "Not again!"

With that she ran out of the mall and to her car where started to cry.

The next morning, Bob went to Julia's office to find out why he was stood up at the shopping mall yesterday.

He sensed coolness as he entered. Everyone seemed to de glaring at him. Obviously, Julia had told everyone about the episode at the mall.

"Hi," he said with a cheerful voice. He started to ask about yesterday but could see that Julia seemed to be upset.

"If you are going to ask why I didn't meet you yesterday, just ask Sandi. I am sure she would have something nice to say," she said that not even looking at him. Then she looked up at him and continued, "I saw you Sandi holding hands."

Bob shook his head as if to clear it. Then thought for a moment and remembering what had happened with Sandi.

"If you had stayed a moment longer, you would have witnessed an ugly scene. I jerked my hand back and stomped out leaving her facing a lot of curious close by diners. It was just an unfortunate, accidental meeting between us. I'm sorry," He added and started for the door.

Anita ran over to Julia, grabbed her arm and dragged her to Bob before he reached the door.

They looked at each other and started to laugh.

The gals actually started to applaud.

Julia was passing Bob's office after making a delivery close by, and as always, she poked her head in to wave and say Hi.

"Oh, good," he said getting up and going out to meet her. "I was thinking that it's about time we did the 'restaurant thing'. What to you think?'

"Sounds great to me," she said.

"Then it's a date," he said, "Pick you up about five thirty?"

"How about we just meet there separately like we did the first time," she asked. The idea had just popped into her mind.

"Even better still," he said, "make it six."

At six o'clock, they were at the restaurant door. Bob opened it and said, "After you."

Julia said, "Deja vu.," as she entered.

There was the usual cheers from the locals who knew them while all others wondering what that may have been about.

They were escorted to their usual booth.

Sally came over with the water glasses. She put one of the glasses in front of Bob and said, "I made yours especially wet."

He looked over to Julia and said, "She's never going to let me live that down, is she?"

"She always did have a good memory," Julia commented.

While they were waiting for their salmon, Bob said, "There was a method to my madness about being here tonight."

"Oh," Julia said looking concerned.

"Yeah, I need to ask you something," he said in a serious manner.

"Yes," Julia blurted out.

"Huh?" Bob asked.

"Yes," she repeated.

"I haven't asked anything yet," he said.

"Oh, I'm sorry. Go ahead.

He reached into his pocket and pulled out a beautifully decorated ring box. He opened it and displayed a spectacular diamond ring.

"Yes," she said.

"Will you just wait until I ask you something?" he said looking impatient.

He took the ring out of the box, held it up and said, "Julia, you would make me the happiest guy in the world, if you would be my wife. Will you?"

There was a long pause.

"You can say 'yes' now," he said.

"YES," was her reply.

She held out her left hand and he slipped it onto her ring finger. It was a perfect fit.

She held her hand up, adjusted the ring and said," It is so beautiful."

Bob said, "Yeah, I lucked out. It was on special at the jewelry counter at Walmart for $59.95.

Julia dropped her hand and said,"Yeah, right"

Bob picked up the box, looked at it, and said, "However this box cost six thousand seven hundred, four dollars and seventeen cents."

"Seventy cents?" she quipped as a come back.

"Yeah, that was almost a deal breaker," he said still looking at the box.

Just then, Sally came up and started to say, "How about some des….." She stopped short after seeing the open ring box and said, "OK, where's the contents of that box?"

Julia held up her left hand and said, "Right here."

After the oohs and aahs, she turned to Bob and said, "So you finally made your quasi fiancée a real fiancée." Then added, "It's about time."

She turned around and yelled, "They are engaged!"

A huge cheer went up and some of the ladies ran over to see the ring and bestow congratulations

Bob cowered back into the corner of the booth and crossed his arms.

After the 'dust cleared' and every one left, Julia and Bob just sat there looking at each other.

Bob asked Julia," What are you thinking about?

"Dates," Julia, answered without hesitating.

"Why would you think about fruit at a time like this", He asked.

"No, silly. Wedding dates," she said then realizing that he was kidding. "When do you think it should be?" she asked as she looked again at the ring.

"Midnight too soon?" he asked.

Sure, why not," she quipped.

When Julia got to her office on Monday, she was not aware that word had gotten out about the good news.

All the girls with questions, questions and more questions mobbed her.

"Whoa," She said, "I am still trying to make sense of all this myself. If you are asking about the date; it all depends when my mom and dad can find the time."

She should realize that her parents would drop anything when they would get the word.

The next time she saw Bob, she said, "Well, I guess we missed that midnight we talked about. How about we make in on June 22nd. That's only a couple of weeks from now but, like any girl, I have been planning this since about the about the age of three and I am ready to go!"

"Wow, that's a lot to have on your mind all these years," he said in bit of a shocked tone.

"Build in female mentality," she said. "I will contact mom and dad to see if the date will suit them," she added.

"Let me know and I will make the travel arrangements," Bob said. "I will get word to the brothers. Would love to see their faces when they get the news," he added.

Turns out that they were expecting the news and wondered why it took so long.

Frank and Helen along with boys as well as some of Bob's close friends flew in from Detroit.
Nana Velma was with them.
Mike, Barbara and son arrived later that day.
They were all staying at the Biltmore.
Bob checked in also so he could be with them most of the time.
Roy Montgomery came in the following day and checked into the Biltmore as.well. Katherine had come in a few days earlier to help Julia with the planning.
Julia and Bob played host that night with a meal at the Point Of View restaurant in South Mountain.

The big day finally arrived and found Bob and his brothers together in the sacristy of the church doing last minute adjustments.
Frank and Mike were standing in as double best men.
The minister poked his head in and signaled that was about time to get the 'show on the road'.
They went out and took their proper place near the alter rail. Bob looked out at all the smiling faces and was wondering who all those people were. He did not realize they had so many friends.
Katherine was seated in the first row of the bride's side. The empty seat next to her was for Roy who would be walking Julia down the aisle.

There were two empty seats in the first row of the groom's side. One had a father's boutonnière on it and on the other, a mother's corsage.

Nana Velma was seated in the next space.

The three brothers looked at the two empty seats with sad expressions.

Back in the foyer, the wedding procession was assembling. Sally was Julie's maid of honor and Anita along with Helen and Barbara were the bride's maids. The girls from Julia's office lined up along both sides of the aisle as honor guards.

Julia's dad was dressed in the full dress uniform of a police chief.

He reached into his pocket and pulled out his handcuffs.

Julia looked down with a silent question.

He smiled and snapped one side on her wrist.

Then snapped the other side on his wrist. He looked at Julia and smiled.

She thought, "OooKay"

The wedding march began and the whole procession started down the aisle.

Everyone stood.

When Julia and her dad reached Bob, he looked down at the shackled Julia and her dad and looked a little shocked.

Roy reached down, unlocked his side of the cuffs then took Bob's arm and snapped it on his wrist.

Then with a broad smile said, "She's all yours.

Bob accepted with that a smile and Roy sat down with Katherine.

Bob looked at Julia who just shrugged her shoulders.

It was a typical ceremony with all the usual vows and instructions.

As usual, the final line for the minister was, "Now with the authority vested in me, I now pronounce you man and wife, you may kiss the bride."

They looked into deep into each other's eyes and placed a warm tented kiss on their lips.

Then they looked down at the handcuffs and said together,

"What just happened here?"

Then Bob said, "I hope your dad gave you the key."

Julia just said, "Wouldn't you just like to know."

Donna and Arnie Gilson are a retired couple living in the pine forest surrounded town of Payson, in what is known as the Rim Country of Arizona. Their saying is,

"We may be two people, but we are one individual."

Made in the USA
Columbia, SC
02 February 2020

87392724R00048